FOUR DIRECTIONS

MITRAJIT BISWAS

Made with ♥ on the Notion Press Platform
www.notionpress.com

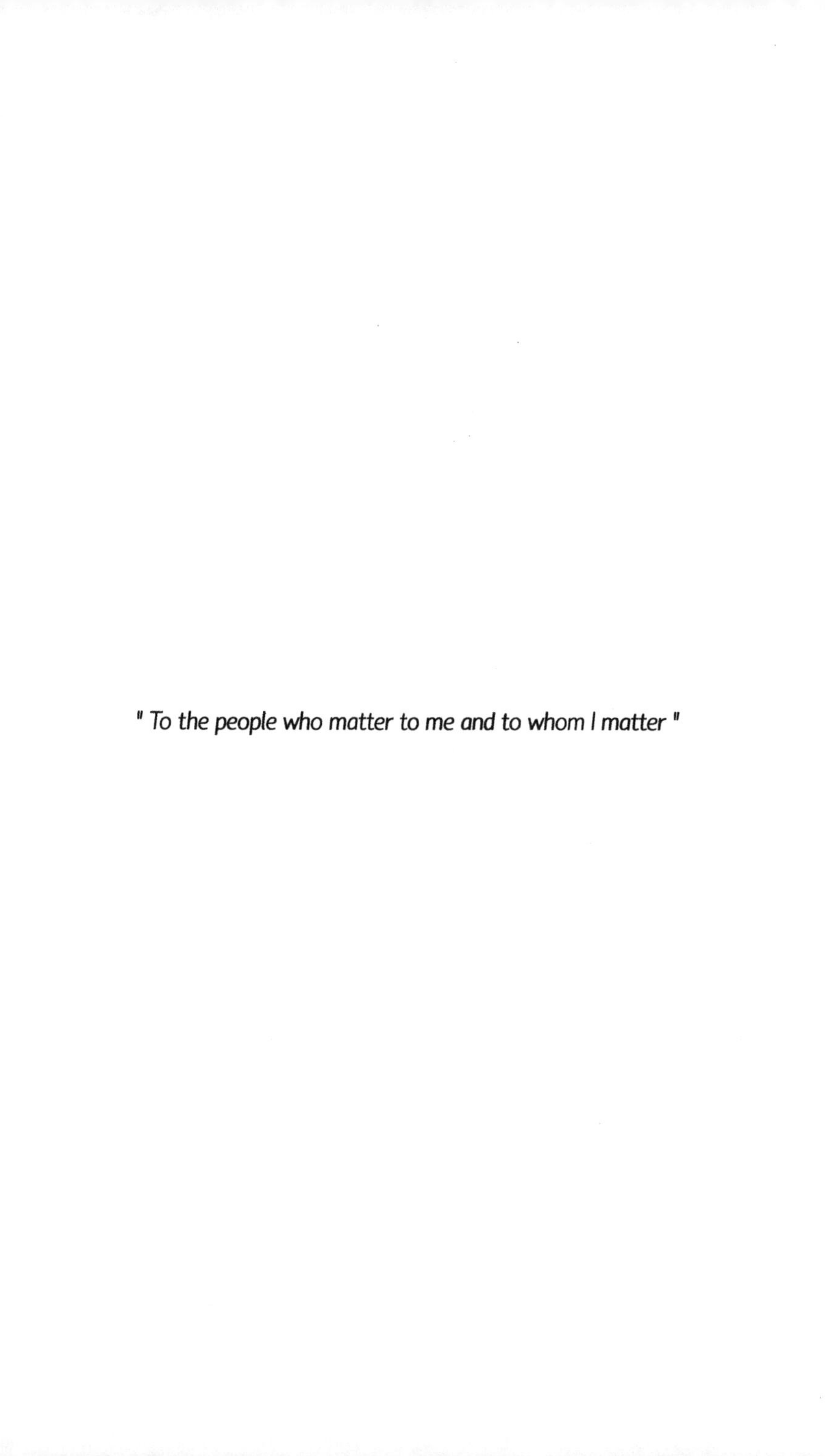

" To the people who matter to me and to whom I matter "

Contents

Preface

A culmination of four short stories of different flavours.

Introduction

Mitrajit also wanted to be known by his nom de plume "Norwester" is passionate about travelling, writing and learning new things.

CHAPTER ONE

Strumming out of the air with broken guitar strings

In one corner of the small dingy room, Deotima was sitting with her broken guitar. She had been practicing with this electric guitar of her brother for the last two years. The laptop screen was open. A playlist of some of the biggest Air-guitar videos filled the history of his viewing. It has been in her dream since her brother passed away in a car accident mysteriously. The family since then had been a broken piece. Deotima's brother, Agniban had been missing from the family in terms of the joy and the happiness he used to bring. Deotima and Agniban were two years with Deotima being elder. She was a lawyer by profession and her brother Agniban had just entered a digital news agency "M-Powered".

The parents were always supportive of both of them. Dad was a homeopathic doctor and Mom a teller at Union Bank of India. Life was happy and good for them until the day of 23rd June, 2017 changed their lives forever. Agniban had been promoted to the position of executive editor for the division of crime and politics-related stories. He was getting caught up all day in his work of looking up and chasing stories involving murder, rape, political controversies, and organized crime. Amidst all of this his passion in terms of his jamming with his amateur music band "Norwester" was taking a back seat. Also, he always dreamt to represent India someday to become the winner of World Air Guitar Championship held in the USA.

Agniban had been working on an investigative report related to a mining-related murder and political struggle in the western part of the state. He liked to keep work to himself but over the period of his last few days he was caught up in his work. In fact, he did not return home for a period of three months before he could make time for a family holiday which happened to be his last. He was killed in an accident at Siliguri from where they were planning to move to Darjeeling. The painful part was to give his body away for the post-mortem which caused a severe breakdown in the family. However, Deotima had stayed strong with the car owner arrested that hit him when he was crossing hill cart road. Initially, there was nothing to prove that any foul play had been involved and the car driver was let go. Deotima still believed that her brother had been taken away from her because of a big conspiracy. She had joined a law firm to understand the law better and secretly she hoped for fighting and investigating the deep underlying truths which may be hidden holding the answers to her brother's untimely demise. She had gone through some of the reports that her brother published for his news agency. Names of some of the local ruling party MLA's were mentioned. Deotima used to clutch her fingers with discomfort whenever she read those reports thinking if she could have warned her brother earlier.

She had filed for a case reopening in 2019 for which she used to be summoned at Lal bazar. She was asked to visit the Lal bazar police station as there have been some new developments which had come to the notice. She went from her chambers directly to the police headquarters where Arunodhay Biswas the inspector in charge of this specific case was waiting to meet her. She was naturally very curious to know what were the latest developments. The inspector told her that the person who was let go being involved in the accident of your brother recently was shot dead. That too after being involved in an accident near Kolkata and being on the run for about a week. Initially, there were no police complaints but the body of this driver Santu Das who killed Asif Sheikh in another accident came to the forefront, He was killed at Barasat involving a local land mafia. The interesting fact is that your brother's reports on M-Powered talking about a specific MLA also has connection with the local councillor supposed to be involved here. The officer continued to say while looking at me. I did not know how to react as I was honestly impressed by the police detective. I was wondering whether there was really a hope for my brother to get justice finally. The police detective told me that he would try his best to find more leads as he said I would be called.

As I came out walking out of the room, in the back of my mind I knew that it was time for me to visit the places of Santu Das and Asif Sheikh. I knew I just could not wait for the police to work for me as it was also my duty to avenge my brother. Thinking of avenging my brother I realized that the Air Guitar Championship, India selection round was in the next two months and I did not know if I was really prepared for the trials. I knew that I had to reach home early and get on with my online classes. Time was short and every moment was important whether it was about catching the real culprits whom my brother was trying to expose or be it for the Air Guitar Championship. The national trials would be held in Pune in the next two months and I knew that it was not going to be easy. A girl who had only seen her brother play the guitar during his gigs and jamming session has now suddenly picked it up and that too Air Guitar just to feel that I can play a role towards helping my departed brother's dreams. The question I used to keep on asking myself was that was I doing it just to make myself feel better morally and provide an outlet for my family. Can it really bring me peace if I make it to the Air Guitar Championship?

With all of these thoughts back in my mind, I was back to my home and went back to the store room where my brother used to spend most of his time. I redecorated it with the things he used to like. Posters of Liverpool FC and East Bengal had been put up. He was big on global politics and therefore a big world map was placed on the centre. The room was still dingy but for me, it had a lot of memories. I did not allow my parents to visit the room as I knew that in the back of my mind they would be torn apart. My online classes allowed me to not only focus on the readapted passion of my brother into mine but also experience something new. It was a newfound passion that drove me away from the constant soul searching of my life after my brother's demise. My practice used to go on from 8 P.M. till 10 P.M. and then I would sit for my own practice in front of the big mirror. The broken Electrical Guitar which I was using to practice for the Air Guitar Championship was also a bundle of memories for me. The guitar was with him when the truck him and he was carrying it. The Guitar had broken strings and a crack right across the centrepiece but it still survived. Although the Guitar neck did survive my brother could not and yet as they say move on.

I knew I had to visit the house of Santu Das and Asif Sheikh and what were their connection to the question of looking into how my brother was killed. I knew that to get the address of both of them, I had to get the details of their family location from the inspector and most importantly it was going to be difficult to determine if they were still there. I gave a call to the inspector of the detective department, Lal bazar. The call went unanswered but after a few minutes around 12:30 P.M. when my parents had gone off to sleep and I was strumming with the guitar in my room I received a text. It read come and meet me tomorrow which was a Saturday at a cafeteria in north Kolkata. He was off duty tomorrow and he would be able to answer any questions off the record. I knew that I had to get the address and undertake the journey by the next two days. My intuition was telling me that their family members may already have been threatened and it was not going to be easy to get information for them. Yet it was the option I had. Amidst all of these thoughts and how soon I can access information from the inspector and if I can actually get information from them which would help me to make headway, I had fallen asleep. It was only when my alarm went off at 6 A.M. I woke up startled.

I knew that it was now time to take the next step. I was about to meet inspector Biswas when I received a call. The call said that don't meet the inspector else your life would be in trouble. I did not know what to make of that call in terms of it being a threat or the one of concern. The true caller app on my phone showed it to be a call with the name Bangla. It did not make any sense and I knew I had to see inspector Biswas's assistance. I do not know if

I was looking for too much help from him but in the back of my mind, I saw him as a man who can help me. I was on my way to meet him as he asked me to meet around 1 P.M. I did not want it to be too much of a conversation as I wanted the information so I could be out with my own mission. I reached the cafeteria that he asked me to come to but he was not there. After waiting for about 10 mins as I was about to call him, he finally arrived. He apologized for being slightly late and then he sat down. He looked around to find out that whether anybody was there. I started and told him that I received a call from someone who told me not to meet you.

I added that on checking the number on the number finder app it showed the number "Bangla". Inspector Biswas told me that he would look up for the number. Then he told me that he is going to accompany me off duty to visit the homes of Santu and Asif. He however said that he had to be careful because some other senior officers are also involved in the investigation. However, I told him that I wanted to go tomorrow itself and I cannot wait for a few more days. Arunodhay told me not to venture alone as it could be risky and I could be targeted. I said that I know the risks but I need to go ahead. He looked at me and I don't know what he saw in my eyes or probably the determination on my face that he said he would accompany day after tomorrow. He said I assure you that give me one more day and I will go with you. I did not know if this could be said that he was going out of the way to help me and if he had any motive. I told him that I did not want to waste a single more day as I took the sip of my coffee. He paused for a while and then he said, we will visit their village tomorrow morning itself. I was quite surprised to find out that he agreed as we then discussed on whom to visit first and other plans for the visit.

We decided to leave tomorrow morning as I had taken a leave for a week. The address of Santu and Asif were of two adjoining villages at Barasat on the outskirts of Kolkata. Inspector Biswas had arranged for a car that would take us there. We were supposed to go from Sealdah station as we wanted to start early. The difficult part was that there were local police who were observing their homes including the MLA's house since the incident came to light in many newspapers. This all started with the news being reported on the news portal M-Powered. After those police visited us once my brother was snatched away from us. However, the real pressure began to build up when this news was picked up by another journalist Asif Sheikh who died near his office in a similar road mishap late at night. It was after three days that the driver of the van was identified as Santu Das who by that time had been reported to be missing. It was after a week that his decomposed body was found from a brick kiln. Through all of these incidents the connection to the ruling party MLA who was the son of a former government contractor was coming up. The pressure was building up and the local police as well as Kolkata police got involved. I was lost in all of these thoughts as by the time we had nearly reached Barasat. We were headed for the house of Asif Sheikh first.

I was carrying a recorded and a small pin button camera which belonged to my brother initially. We managed to reach his home after some asking. We could spot a few local policemen there. Inspector Biswas looked at me perplexed. I told him that let me try if I can find some information. After waiting for a while, I went up to his home and as I was about to enter Asif's home I was stopped by a local constable. I showed my lawyer ID card and said I belong to an NGO and was here for legal discussion. He looked at one of his seniors who after looking at me called up his senior. I do not what was said to him but he looked at me I can meet his wife for 5 minutes. I hurriedly entered the room as the car was left behind. I came back to the car and said to Inspector Biswas that if the local police ask anything about you, say that you are from the NGO. I managed to get a glimpse of Asif's wife and mother along with his 6-year-old daughter. I knew that I had to be sensitive and gave me story in brief withholding some information. I asked her three questions as I knew my time would be up. How long has her husband been a journalist? Did he know Santu Das? Was he threatened by the local MLA before in terms of his work?

She replied that she did not know her husband was in any kind of trouble until recently before his death he came running. He was using his mobile phone and then he seemed to be in a panic mode. He took out a small thing from his phone like a sim card. I understood that she was referring to a memory card and then he put it in an envelope. I asked her where was that. She replied that it was with her at her bank locker. I could not ask her more as the police had arrived by then and asked that I should leave. I replied firmly that I am not yet done and I needed another 10 minutes at least. The constable did not seem to like the reply but waited outside. I told him to stand away from the door as he got angry and then he moved away slightly. I went up to Asif's wife and asked her that can she arrange the memory card as it would help both of us in our fight. She said that she would try to get it but she was scared that she may be followed in the bank. However, there was determination in her eyes as I held her hand. I could sense that she wanted to help me and believed in me. As for the other two questions I had asked her, she replied no and yes respectively as I got her number before leaving.

Next, it was my turn to visit the home of Santu Das who was in the adjoining village. I came back to the car and inspector Arunodhay clearly wanted me to answer a lot of questions. I told him to hold his horses as time was important. Inspector Biswas told me that he was famished and so was I however we could not waste time. Our car rushed towards the house of Santu Das. It was not difficult to find his home as he was well known to be the best driver of the local MLA in his commercial enterprises. The ones that included coal mining, timber, sand and raw materials for construction. He had made a name for himself and was doing well for himself until the accident happened. This is what was said by the locals as here the police picket around his home seemed laxer. I do not know the reason for that however it did make my job easier or so I thought. There were a few local party officials who were keeping a watch on his place which I did not realize in the beginning. As soon as I tried to enter Santu's home I was surrounded by the party officials and two policemen. They came to the car and threatened us. I don't know how inspector Biswas kept calm but I managed to stick to the story of being from a Law NGO although still that did not help me to enter house of Santu.

His wife was definitely there but I was stopped by the local party officials and the cops who did not want me to get close. It was a bit too apparent oddly but I knew that this could happen. I was not disappointed me as my real victory now would lie in getting access to the memory card that Asif had left behind. That was the main onus for me which can signify that at least whatever I wanted to accomplish here can begin from that. The only real worry was to access the material. That is something that I wanted to look into later. As for now I was hungry and was desperately looking for a place to eat. The local goons and the police chased our car until we left the vicinity as after a while Arunodhay spoke. He said you took me all the way here as I tagged along but I stayed cooped up in this car along with this driver. The driver by the way just because he is personally known to me continued Inspector Biswas is why he agreed to be here. I thanked the driver named Krishna as I wondered whether he really was playing the role of his namesake deity and driving us all the way up to here. We reached for a local food joint somewhat away from Santu's place. It occurred to me in a long time that the basic instincts of life are what people forget is the most important despite the quest for the power and glory.

We were having lunch when I told Inspector Biswas of my next plan of action. He was definitely appalled when I told him about all of that. I told him that I would stay here around Asif's home and sneak into his room by tonight. Initially, Inspector Biswas looked at me and asked me if I was being silly or was, I actually looking to commit this stupidity. Once he was convinced that I was stubborn about doing it, he asked me how was I planning to stay the night or rather wait till the sunset. I said that I would wait around a local temple that I had seen at the center of the village. Then around 8:30 P.M. the time by which the village should be asleep, I am going to sneak into Asif's home. Inspector Biswas probably controlled his bemusement and slight anger as well. Then he looked at me and said this is the last thing I am going to be a part of for now. Tonight because of you, I will stay back and asked the driver to stay back. His rank in the detective department definitely did give him the edge and I was not feeling guilty at all for using him, I knew that I had to get to the bottom of this and this memory card was the key to all of it. We parked our car on the outskirts of his village and waited.

Around the time of dusk, we stepped out of the car. Inspector Biswas said that he will follow me from a distance. The low lights adorned the newly paved roads of this village as we moved closer to the home of Asif. I could spot that there was a small shed near the temple where we could wait. Approximately around half an hour later finishing our dinner with the plastic tiffin box that we carried it was time to move closer towards his home. It took us around 10 minutes to reach his home as even the cell tower showed three bars still it did work here. Last time I had saved the location on my mobile phone google maps. I saw two policemen speaking amongst themselves. Inspector Biswas asked me what exactly was the plan. I said that I would try to sneak into Asif's house, speak to her wife and ask her to send me the memory card from the local post office. Inspector Biswas said this was your plan all along. The first part can be still done but as for the second part how do you expect her to get it from the bank locker by tonight. I replied that I did not expect her to give me the memory card by tonight. I wanted her to pick it up and send me across that at an appropriate time to my place through you. Inspector Biswas was dumbstruck but I was desperate enough to try out everything.

Ultimately, he asked me how was I supposed to get it. I told him that after speaking to Asif's wife I would ask her the exact date and time within the next two days. You will go to the bank on the same day and wait to look to open a new account for an NGO. Then she will draw out the memory card from the locker and hand it to you. Inspector Biswas asked if I had been watching too many movies? I ignored the response and at that moment I saw an opening to enter Asif's home as the policemen left to wash their hands behind the temporary shed. Inspector Biswas waited at the turn of the road. It was about 10 minutes as the policemen were smoking and had their back turned towards me or rather the entrance. I sneaked out and ran with slow but steady steps. My heart was beating so fast that I could hear it as I approached Inspector Biswas and told him that I had been able to convey my message. The rest was up to us and Gayatri. We walked steadily up to the car which was kept behind a tree on the field and waited till 2 A.M. approximately. Our car started as we reached Kolkata. Two days later as I was in my room around 6 P.M. in the evening back to holding that broken guitar with quivering fingers I got a call from Inspector Biswas sounding resoundent!

CHAPTER TWO

The Blue Diary

The soiled pages of a blue leather diary read "1943". The train was moving on as I flipped through the pages. It was the memoir of my Great grandfather passed to my father and I just received it from him two days back during my birthday. I was the fourth generation in my family to have joined the army and I was home during my annual holidays. My grandfather was in the armed forces of British India and was sent to Africa and later to Italian and German front. However, this diary was my family legacy for something else. The first chapter I was going through starts when the British forces were defeated and taken as P.O.W. by Africa Corps of Rommel. My great grandfather named Sardar Ajitesh Singh along with his 400 compatriots were stationed in Berlin. For the first time there he had heard the speech of Netaji on Berlin Radio who was inviting all the prisoners of war to join the cause of fighting for India or the idea of India. The diary has been written in Gurumukhi but the language and the flow made it easy for me to reconnect with my country and family's past. It was the onset of the year 1942 and somewhere I had heard that Nazi Germans were torturing the local people as well others. The next line that read gave me goosebumps. "Thinking of all this I was thinking whether I was a free man myself and fighting for what?".

I was trying to reconnect not only with my family's past but also with the past of my nation. I turned the next pages. The prisoners of war were taken to a centre nearby where the volunteers of Indian Legion were roaming around. This was my first tryst with an Indian organization operating in Europe. While reading it, I was thinking that may be my grandfather had forgotten about the Ghadar party which was one of the first organization operating against the Raj. However, skipping that thought aside I started reading the diary again. He was sitting on a bench with a form written in German and he could not understand what to do and where to go. The Indian legion members were absolutely nowhere to be seen. It was later times of 1942 and the weather was freezing. I saw a lady walking up to me. I don't know what she said. However, then she took the form out my hands, looked at it and then signalled for a pen. I gave her a pen. She filled it up and then gave me back the form. As she was about to leave I could only understand that she said India and then she wrote in my hand a location. I could not read or write much of English as I knew that I had to ask my friends or Legion members as my commanding British officers were all imprisoned. I could only say thank you as she left.

It was about one month later during the time that I had finally decided to join in the Indian Legion. Just before the handover ceremony I had discovered that it was a nearby location. The officers of the Indian Legion gave me a rough idea of the housing barrack as mentioned in the location. I wanted to meet this lady before I left. I reached around evening and saw a small house with an open veranda. Outside the home I saw a sign marked with a yellow star. I did not understand back then. I tried to look in for anything but could not. I was about to leave as I knew that lurking around in an enemy territory was not suited. As soon as I started walking, I noticed a boy running towards me. He gave me a letter and then ran away; I could not ask him for anything. Three days had passed by and by that time I had finally showed the letter to only person who was my Indian superior named Parameshwar Das. The letter read that if he had received the letter from a boy then probably, they will never meet again. It read further that she had been always fascinated about India having read the books and heard about it. She had met a few other Indian soldiers but was really fascinated by me because of my Turban and the different look I carried. She had been probably taken to a place of no return.

The last paragraph read that she would like a part of her to visit India. My great grandfather could not make sense that what did she mean by a place of no return. Parameshwar said that he had heard about concentration camps where the Jewish people were taken away. They were never seen again. Then there was a gap of a page. Again, the writing started. It was after a gap of one month. My great grandfather had joined the Indian Legion but he was still in Berlin. He had not been able to join the on-ground troops in Asia. He had been looking for information about this mysterious woman who gave her this letter. After a search it was found out that she was named Amanda Feydrich. She had been there for the last 10 years nearly. However, no one in the neighbours knew her parents, they only knew she was a member of the ruling party. No one had also seen her being taken away. My great grandfather tried to contact the nearest civil population register who refused to share information. Although they gave him a very important information that she used to work at a local steel factory as shift manager. I got the name and I figured out the workplace. The war was picking up and the factory owner flatly refused to meet me, However the patience of two days finally bore fruit. It was after two days I could meet the manager to seek information.

He said that the family had been moved to the nearest city relocation place. My grandfather writes that could not understand which place but I had sensed by then this could be places where they were either tortured or something horrible. After about frantic search for the answers finally I got some answers. They were taken away most likely towards Poland. However, I had no idea how to reach there. I was getting engrossed by the story of my grandfather. The pages had turned brittle but the essence of the story kept me going on. My grandfather wanted to start on the journey to meet this woman. However, he wrote before that there were a lot of difficulties. He was a part of Indian Legion and was granted amnesty only because he was a part of it. His official identity was now as a soldier who was fighting for India or about to. He could not leave his mission although he wanted to meet this woman. If he left for India then he knew that it would not be possible to meet her. Also, permission from our supreme commander was needed for the step I wanted to take. After about 10 days I got an appointment with Netaji. I told him that I wanted to stay back in Germany and help here with the local efforts of Indian Legion. Netaji had a bemused look even amongst all his stress as he asked that if I could speak in German or English. I said neither.

He looked at me with a mix of bemusement and annoyance. Then he called me by the name and asked me that how did I expect to help for the local efforts here, I said, Netaji find me any role and I will be of service.

It was to my surprise that he never asked me that why was I not looking to go back to India. He said that his secretary will get back to me as I was asked to provide my details. In the meanwhile, the sections of Indian Legion were being given duties and certain platoons were being asked to prepare to move towards Asia on to the Japanese front. My grandfather meanwhile was waiting for the instruction on where to go next. A memo came two days later where I was assigned duty to be on the lookout for Allied Forces especially the British movements. I was told that I would be given training and sent on deputation towards Poland. My heart skipped a beat although I did not know where to exactly go in Poland. I had a fair idea that it could be Auschwitz. I did not know what it was however I had heard that the Nazi Germans had created a sort of prison where a large number of people were shifted. They were mostly anti-establishment. I made my way towards Poland as the war had already picked up. It was already difficult to move around amidst the ongoing war.

However, in the chilly winter morning, I was assigned with the Indian Legion forces and 20 German officers to reach out to Poland. The irony is that I could not tell the Germans that I wanted to visit Auschwitz. I kept on going with them until the truck stopped near the German frontline. The entire sky was red. After I got down from the truck, I could see the entire sky red in colour because of the aerial battles that had been going on there. I waited for the convoy truck to leave as I was asked to change my outfit and get into civilian clothes. I was asked to report 15 kilometres away from Warsaw. My duty was to look for Russian solider positions dressed as British Overseas force. I was given two identities. If I was stopped by German soldiers then I would show them my Indian Legion card which was sealed in my boots. As for the Russians and the allied forces my narrative was prepared that I was sent here on a recon mission to collect information to send in more troops in the east when possible. I was provided with some information just so that in case, I was apprehended by any of the forces I could give them a cover story. However, I had other plans of my own. I tried to figure out that how far was Auschwitz from this place. I knew I needed to visit there as soon as possible.

It was around afternoon and I was given a bag which contained a few dry food items and a flask of water. I did not report to my official station immediately. I was provided a map. Although I was not that well read but my military training had made me an expert in map reading. I did not know if I could meet her in Auschwitz and what it was all about. Still, I had made up my mind that I would reach there. I did not have much language skills either in German or Polish and the map showed that I am still 45 kilometres away from Auschwitz. Moving till there with my Indian Legion pass would not be difficult but the trek was risky. The main risk involved how to move through the enemy fire and get close to the place at Auschwitz, I started following the map and although it was getting dark, I decide that I needed to cover at least 10 kilometres somehow. There was risk of getting caught up in the fire. Overall time was short. I started to move along the muddy trail and the rubble although it was pretty dark. I knew that I could not carry for long as I hardly could see anything. The time for me was now to find a safe space but being a brown guy in Europe of those times was not easy. I had read till now when my father called me for dinner.

My dad asked me how was finding the diary. I just looked at him and said, that how come I was not told about this important part of my family history. My dad replied that he wanted it to be a surprise. One part of my heart wanted to ask my dad how the story ended. Whereas the other part of my heart wanted to finish the story on my own. I looked to quickly finish my dinner and then get back to reading the remaining part of the story. I went back to my sleeping room and took back the diary, I got immersed in the story once again. The voice of my grandfather seemed to echo as I read that he waited at a nearby tavern which was half broken. He was given refuge by the German soldiers who were on the lookout for allied forces especially the Russians and the British agents too. They asked him where was he posted, He knew that he could not say that he was posted towards Warsaw as it was already posted. In terms of European Geography as well he was not well versed. He said that he was looking to pass messages abut enemy positions as he was not given a fixed front to report to. After spending the night there, he had deciphered that he was around 30 kilometres away from the Auschwitz area. The British air forces were going through nightly raids as the German Air forces were chasing them.

The aerial battles had turned the skies completely red. Amidst the rubble and the ditches I kept moving on. I was told by the German officers that I may get a ride from the German moving forces showing my ID card. I knew I had to hitch one ride so that I could save time, If I was found out that I was not performing my duties it would be a matter of shame and dishonour personally and professionally and there was a risk of being disowned as well. I had barely moved 1 kilometre away from the tavern when I was stopped by a German Corporal. He asked me in German first and then switched to English as to what was I doing here, I showed him my ID card and told him my duty was to report on British agents as well as Russian forces.

He nodded and said that he will give mc a lift. He asked me where should I drop him. I calculated that I needed to tell him a location close to Auschwitz but not the precise location. I had observed a location on the map I was carrying and told him who was named Olaf Schwitz. He had been posted here for the past two years and was under direct command of the SS. The name struck a chord as I remembered that they were the same group who were probably rounding up the Jews and some other people as well.

I told him of the spot which was exactly 10-12 kilometres away from Auschwitz. The corporal seemed a bit surprised but was probably in a bit of hurry. He was quite skilled in the way he was riding the bike amidst the muddy trail. He carried on and took me up to the spot as he himself was headed in that direction. It was much later that I would get to know that this was not the only tryst that I was going to have with him. It was around late afternoon that I had finally reached the spot. The skies were red but the sun peaked through giving a bit of respite in the biting cold of around March. He dropped me off and said goodbye as he went off. I waited for a while as I could see a small village around. I decided I had to take the step forward as I walked up to the village. There was no one around as I finally came around a home. I knocked on the door and out came an old lady. I thought she would close the door. I asked for a glass of water gesturing with my hands. I don't know what she could understand however she brought me inside. I could see a few old German furniture and paintings apart from two-three bullet holes as well. She brought me a glass of water and two pieces of bread. She did not speak much but merely kept looking at me.

After I put the pieces of bread in my bad and drank the water quickly, I bowed down my head and left. As soon as I was leaving from the door. I could hear fire shots. The lady behind me did not seem terrified as I could hear a few sheep bleat. She calmly closed the door as I could hear gun shots which was probably around 700 meters away. The calmness of the place made the sound seem right there in front of my ears as well as the eyes. I decided to follow the sound of the gun fire. It took me around 5 minutes when I saw a column of German soldiers retreating as there were British and most likely US soldiers marching ahead. I was surprised to see the US forces as I was told to be on the lookout for British soldiers but not the US ones. Also, I did not see any Russian soldiers. I had made up my mind on what to do. I was going to use my British India forged ID card. I met them as the army trucks was crossing the German posts which now remained empty. One of the British soldiers popped a question in English. I found comfortable at least for then in the company of my colonizers. I asked him where were they were heading. They said they were heading towards Auschwitz. My heart skipped a beat. I showed them my British Indian soldier ID and was offered a lift in the truck.

As the truck moved on the muddy trail we started speaking. I could not tell the British soldiers that I was a part of Indian Legion. I had to pretend that I was a part of the Allied force. Basically, I was caught up in a catch 22 situation. I decided to stick to the story of being an agent of the British Indian forces who was sent from France to lookout for possible German positions in Poland and report back to London. As for the US soldiers they were from places such as New York, Connecticut, Los Angeles. I had never heard about these names before until someone showed me a picture of New York. The US soldiers seemed more friendly as they offered me biscuits. They were curious to know about India to which I could not reply much in details and freely. There was a kind of shame and guilt as I felt for the first time the suffocation of being a nation which you can't call your own. Meanwhile the sun had nearly set. It was pitch dark as the truck stopped. The soldiers at the back asked what happened. The driver replied "We have come close to the Auschwitz Camp". A thick smoke was bellowing out as we could see. The US solider gave me a spare standard issue kept in the truck and asked me to join them. I finally realized that now I was a part of this group and marched alongside them.

The US air forces could be heard from the skies as we treaded along. The walk lasted for about an hour. After a duration as Prisoner of War in Germany, I finally felt that I was back in the war. However, my soul was torn between the question of where do I stand ideologically. Amidst all these thoughts we reached near the gates of Auschwitz. A thick smoke was bellowing out from behind and I could see so many people standing right in front of the gates. They all looked so malnourished. I was second in line as the British and US forces hurriedly entered the camp. It smelled of burnt bodies as I was about to throw up. Amidst all the crowd then suddenly I realized the woman for whom I had come this far. The rest of the group started to gather the survivors as I could see huge pieces of rubble and the blazing fire from the backside of the huge area of this camp. I had no idea that this was what they called "Concentration Camps" and this is what is Auschwitz looks like. My eyes were peeled on for that face. While searching for that face amongst the few hundred suddenly the other soldiers stopped as a door was open where heaps of bodies were found. The stench was unbearable and the survivors pointed to a spot saying there were more as my search rapidly intensified.

After about looking for about half an hour there was one barrack from where the survivors were being brought outside, A few of the soldiers were standing outside but most importantly there was a woman who was no stranger to me. She was the reason that I had crisscrossed across this much of alien territory leaving behind my duty. Once the last of the survivors had been taken over, she came running towards me with her pale face and a skinny frame. In just a few days the soul of her seemed to have been suck dry although her eyes still had that charm and the spark. She spoke in broken English and said she did not how to thank me. I looked up at the sky and showed my finger up there. Meanwhile amidst all of this the US forces found a file contain the name of all key resources and a brief of the daily activities were mentioned there. There was a list of names and something written in German. However, what really caught my eye was that there was the signature of Olaf Schwitz. As I walked outside the small room, I could see her lying on the stretcher. As soon as she saw me she let out her hand as I held it and then she said in a faint voice "Thank you" as she was stretchered out. It was after a week when the Russian soldiers had already entered Poland and was on the verge of taking over Germany. It was only after a day that I heard that three officers from this camp had been arrested by US forces which included Olaf Schwitz.

It was the month of April. Finally, I got her name. She was named Alice. She was born of Jewish parents. Her father had always spoken about India and wanted to visit India. I was happy that she could speak and that too in English which not too bad. She told she could speak about

5 languages including English taught by her father who was later persecuted along with her mother. She could escape but then she was caught being betrayed by one of the neighbours. She said that she would go back with the remaining Jews as they were being relocated to a new place. I told her that I too had to return to my homeland. It was only three days earlier I heard that Netaji had apparently died in a crash and things in India were also fiery. I knew that I had not performed the duties given by Netaji but probably he would have understood my call although no duty is greater than serving the nation. I asked Alice if she would join me on a voyage to India before going to Israel. She smiled and added before that she needed to meet a man who was in charge of death camps here. I asked who was it. She mentioned Olaf Schwitz as the diary ended there.

CHAPTER THREE

The Yellow & Black Strips

Miracle Adventure Tours had a small office in the Kidderpore area of Kolkata. The company offered local tour along with other national and international tours like any travel agency. However, it was not until one of the tours that they organized at Sundarbans 6 months back which brought their company into focus which were not all welcome. A group of 6 people from Kolkata went to Sundarbans during the month of June just before the onset of Monsoons which not only changed the fate of this company but also for the ones who went on that trip to mysterious Sundarbans. The group of 6 people who belonged in the age group of around 18-21 had their own YouTube channel which had around 5 Lakh subscribers and was growing. The channel name "Zeitgeisters" were more into uncovering facts, myths and urban legends. This trip towards Sundarbans was also based on such myth surrounding a left-over map at Hamilton Bungalow which was made by Sir Hamilton containing the details of a place deep in the ravines. It contained details of around two boxes of jewellery that were stolen by Bengali and Portuguese pirates from the Arakan province which is modern day Burma. It is supposedly said as per the reports found in only a few sources that the map may be either in pieces lying around the bungalow or mentioned in one of the belongings at his dilapidated bungalow. The jewellery boxes were lost in a tussle between Bengali and Portuguese pirates.

These two boxes got lost around the mid 1800's as only the remains of the two pirates' boats were found. 7 were dead most likely in the ensuing battle and around a dozen more by the natural surrounding which they could not survive. A report on this was published in the Gazette days after the incident but after that there had been nothing on that. Although it is said the Sir Hamilton had got noted of this fact. The British officers did not want to visit the area whereas Sir Hamilton at that time was looking for means to find that treasure boxes that was in the core forest, It is said that he travelled with a team of around 16 people collected from Gosaba mainly and other places to scout the nearby areas. After a search of two months now and then after the monsoons it is said that he found one of the boats and two boxes. However, he was sure that near the periphery there could be many more treasures which were never found. It is said that he got a significant amount of recovery from the boxes which was used by him for his business and even development purposes around Sundarbans. This report came out in Asian and Bengal gazette but was then never picked up until this bunch of young guys came across it in the archive. Now its time we get back to their story of adventure or misadventure at mysterious Sundarbans delta.

It was the time of the monsoons and the forests were closed. However, these four misfits wanted to utilize this time for the so-called adventure they had planned. They had rented a small trawler that was fit enough to enter the alleys. Overall, the idea for them was to geo locate the topographical map as the area surely had undergone so many changes. The report that they had managed to get from the Asian and Bengal Gazette digital archives version had been now geographically mapped. The plan for the team was to stream it live using portable routers and other military gear they had. However all of this depended on finding the exact location as well possibly trying to locate the present day scenario of that location. A rough periphery of the location where the area was the only thing that this group depended on. Although they had certain other plans up their sleeves which was difficult to execute but not impossible. That is what they depended on. Their journey began amidst the torrential rains when the entire forest area was closed. Rivers in the delta were swollen but they had got a decent sized trawler that they had got from the tour company based on customization. It had satellite towers for communication. Also the design of the boat was designed in a manner that allowed for its bottom part to inflate with rubber paddles. The design inputs was done by Pallika the lone female member and also a Mechanical Engineer.

However before that their idea was to look for a possible left over map about which only speculated based on writings. The writings of Hamilton which was found in one of the archives but has since never been talked about. It is said that the map was hidden in one of the floor basements right at the centre. The bungalow has been renovated but it was definitely possible for the map to be there. It may be soiled, moth eaten or even torn but even if some of the remnants can be found then it could help on their mission. Although the chase could be still elusive however if they could find the map it could still mean a lot. However, they knew they had to be careful as the patrol boats would be around the bungalow. They had a time slot of only 1 hour to 2 hours around early evening to try to look for the map. If they felt they cannot access the map they had a plan to scout for the area which was just away from the core area. They could track boats in the vicinity and everything was ready. The rains had started to pour in as slowly but steadily the boat made way to the bungalow. Hardly a thing was visible but they knew they had to try to get close to the bungalow. The metal detection kit and quick shoving materials were kept ready for the first phase of their exploration.

The water levels were already up the brim of the lower deck and it was indeed to our surprise that we had managed to come up to the river bed adjoining the bungalow. It was raining quote heavily and the main purpose for us was to get to the bungalow and find a way in. Two of our team members which Prakash and Riju got down. Riju had the shovel and Prakash had the electro magnetic scanner. The main question was how to get inside. Our trawler had just managed to get to the side. It was muddy. They tiptoed and saw the door closed. We had calculated that we can get about 1 hour atleast to break in. As decided we had also got a lock cutter and a replacement lock. Riju went up to the door as the visibility was very low. We could only see each other for around 2-3 metres. Prakash helped Riju cut through the lock as it took around 10 minutes. They signalled us that they are going in. We waited as they went in. We did not know what to expect from them as we had to constantly be on the lookout for the patrols and the weather situations. There was a storm brewing and we knew that before we were chased by the patrol groups, we had to move to the location of Gosaba at least till the storm passed away. The atmosphere was as tense as the gloomy skies of the Sundarbans.

We came back to Gosaba island as we had no other option, we knew that the time was crucial but we had to utilize this night. Our team gathered after a quick dinner at a local hotel that we had booked for a month. The idea for us was to get an understanding of the area that we had to look for. There was only hand drawn map that had been scanned and put up along with the article in the digital archive. Now we all looked towards Riju to ask him what he saw in the Bungalow. He said that there was nothing much except for a few photographs and the small knick knacks which were old. However, he said that there could be certain things which may have been there which surely could lead us to something more meaningful. Although we could not depend on that scenario as definitely the incident of the lock being cut would spread around. Although we had managed to put up another smaller lock as a replacement. Still, we knew that time was running out. Our option was to go back to the drawing board literally. This was no corporate meeting but we knew that we were up for some serious business. So we had to look up for the exact area that we were looking to scout for. It has been more than 150 years but the story contained all some extracts of a first hand narrative of the treasure that was lost there.

We managed to pull out the scanned geo-satellite tagged heat map area. We had a plan figured out that where the place we were looking for could be. This could be a small ride island which is close to the Bangladesh waters. There is one particular place where there is an urban legend of a big island chunk that has been said to be submerged during full tide and rises up due to low tide. There were many other smaller islands there which was rich in thick forestation of the area. It is apparently said that those islands were favourite haunt of the pirates as these used to fall in the routes of the traders. We had to figure out that does this fact corroborate with any geographic location. Also we went over the scanned hand drawn map and the article where in the middle few lines talks about the lost treasure possibly containing rare metals used for royal jewellery were hidden there. This account was from an old journal carried by a Portuguese pirate captain. It was originally in Portuguese which was found by a Portuguese Church Priest in Bandel which later got translated into English and Bengali. The area we had to scout for would be far from Gosaba. Our food supply, life boats, satellite functioning would need to be top notch. The risk of being in Tiger territory was real and also not to forget the patrol boats of the rangers on surveillance duty.

Next morning the weather was still grim. We had to venture out and we had prepared a route map. A time frame and patrol boat surveillance tracking were also put into place. The food and the other supplies were also loaded it. This was it. Even if there is a severe storm, wreckage of our customized vessel there is no turning back. We have spent the entire night figuring out the route, cross checked the article. Looked at all the notes for the authenticity of the article. It seemed all elusive but deep down there was a belief that we were venturing deep into the swamp lands of Sundarbans to find something. The storm last night brought torrential rans and the water seemed to be overflowing right up to the brim of our vessel first floor. The route map that had been marked has been done right up to around 100 kilometres away from Gosaba. A deep ride like water path that cuts across the water borders between India and

Bangladesh has lost out on traffic for the last few years. Although occasional trade vehicles such as cement, electronics etc. would travel through this route. However, these probably would not be there during this time of the season. Probably is being used here as later there was something which we did found which was related to a shipping container that we did not expect to find it there. It did change the whole way we looked at our adventure sojourn.

Our destination location was still very much unknown. However, the real deal for this adventure was to find if anything related to the old urban legend. We started early in the morning with the weather still looking grim. The rainfall was pouring in but the winds were not strong enough. We had already got a map with our areas marked where we wanted to venture. It had been around an hour into our journey when we suddenly saw a very old container that may not have been that old. It was probably of a patrol vehicle. However, the fun part is that the shipping container which was stranded there may be more than two years. It would not be wrong to say that the container was here for more than 6 months surely and could hold possibly more information. We took our customized trawler right up to the boat and decided that we need to scan it. Our entire team went ahead as we scouted the entire location. Therc was a lor of excitement and speculation as we stormed in the container whose front part was broken. We went up to the rear part of the ship. Our local boat crew told us that this was a ship from a local export company. However, the ship broke down apparently when it went around a gorge which follows the same path we were trying to go. The ship which was huge drifted away from there on to the main stream with its front broken until it had been towed here and for some mysterious reason the vessel had been here. As soon as we climbed up the local crew said we should be careful. That goes without saying as we all ventured around the vessel. Our localized vessel was about 10 metres away from the marine vessel. I went behind the engine room and started looking around. The steering wheel was covered in oil and grease. I was already curious enough when I found a piece of paper that looked like a soiled paper napkin. It had only a few blackened lines followed by dotted line and coordinates. I did not know if it can be called so convenient but the coordinates did seem familiar to the area we were looking for. I came down with that piece of paper and showed it to my team. They were excited to see that paper. Finally, we decided that this ship needed to be checked especially for the hauls terms of the journey undertaken especially their fateful one. We knew that here we were spending a lot of time, however before we moved ahead this was a god sent intervention for our so-called exploration to get on the right track. The afternoon was approaching and the weather in the next two days was supposed to be windy and rainy. So, we needed to find a spot where we can harbour. This vehicle was used a rear support tied up with our marine vessel immediately.

It indeed did seem weird that with so much preparation we arrived here and then just by mere chance we found a vessel. The vessel that definitely could not be said to be definitely going to the place we were looking for. It could be that maybe one person possibly who was a part of this commercial vessel possibly had idea about this place. The question for us remained that do we decide to follow the coordinates? Are they even close to the place we were looking for or someplace else. The only logical explanation could be that may be it is not the same place. However what else could be so interesting when it comes to coordinates and that too a place like in Sundarbans. All of us were thinking about all of this when the dark clouds started gathering. We knew that we cannot too far ahead. We all settled in the vessel and started looking here and there. The evening set in as we stayed back at the vessel. Our mechanized trawler was already tied with it. The rains started pouring in and I went up to the front deck room. Below the deck was a set of small stairs to which I headed and found a small room. It was stinking of stench and one could barely stand. I switched on my power torch and found that it was a small storage room. It was full of papers which were strewn all over the wooden floor.

The outside wind had started to pick up as the boat started to swing a bit. My feet swayed a bit as I moved closer. I picked up the pieces of paper. The pieces of paper seemed to be from a manuscript. I started picking them up one by one. They were papers which was written beautifully in calligraphic writing. Not only that as I gathered about 50 papers I made them into a bunch and tried to figure out that whether they were arranged chronologically. Once, I was sure enough that there were no more papers and in half an hour the papers had been arranged I came up to the deck above. The tour boat and my other friends looked at me surprised as they had already opened their beer cans and started digging into fried crab. They asked me where I was all this while? I kept mum as I took a beer can. Riju said that winds speeds will increase and here considering the weather and the territory we are parked in the chances of coming face to face with patrol boats was negligible. Yet to avoid risks we had made sure that our trawler was hidden behind the abandoned cargo ship. The hull of the abandoned ship itself was enough to hide our trawler despite being bigger than an average one. I took a piece of fried crab and a can of beer as I moved to the other side of the cargo ship.

I started reading from the pages. The entries started from the month of March 15th. Hamilton wrote that one of his Portuguese friend had visited him in Kolkata. He knew him from his days as a trader and this Portuguese gentleman whose name was not mentioned had been behind the missionary work in Bandel. He was into social work, however there was also a dark past to him. He was one of the notorious pirate gang member and he operated in the western ghats. Until one day he barely escaped with his life in a raid with the local Moplah people. After that he moved to Bengal where he joined the services of Nawab. This was where he had once heard that Shuja left behind a significant amount of wealth in the southern part of Gangetic Bengal. He was chased by pirates from Arakan which I realized is modern day Arakan. In haste he entered one of the creeks of Bengal Sundarbans. His ship had been caught up in storm there and his hull was damaged. However, amidst all of that he did manage to bury two boxes of Mughal state coins which he was carrying with him. The last few lines read that it was on an island which was huge but covered on all sides with thick mangroves, river openings. All of this was witnessed by one of his local followers who had written down the exact description and drawn a rough map. The next part was more interesting,

It read that on the return journey three of them were killed by tigers. However, the map that was drawn came in the possession of Nawab in exile at Kolkata. It is not clear how but it was in his possession. The Portuguese friend of Hamilton visited the Nawab and asked him about the map. The Nawab asked him how he came to know about it. He said that he came to know about it from one of his friends which probably was one of the cooks, The Nawab asked why should he give that map and location to him. Antonio as he was known replied that if he was allowed to go in this expedition, he would return the entire scout to Nawab. The Nawab said he did not have any power as East India company is now in power. He suggested that I speak to Hamilton who was also close to the Nawab. In this manner they both came together and decided to venture out for the hidden treasure. Through this time I had reached around 25 pages through the thick note of papers. Then finally saw the map in a page where the top was soiled. In between I had forgotten about the abandoned ship and how the diary ended up here. The answers to these questions I found them in a while as I quickly glanced over the map and the last remaining few pages of the diary. This is from where our adventure took turn.

The last few pages of the diary had a few notes scribbled in a new kind of ink. The date read 6 months from now on. The name mentioned was Barikul Chowdhury Islam an owner of a shipping company. He mentioned it that he too had read about the article from the internet sources and had looked for an authentic source to get hold of the map if possible. He wrote that in December he found a local contact at a private auction club. This club was originally owned by the son of Antonio. As soon as I turned the page it was back to the old manuscript which continued with the description of the journey. There were two ships. One headed by Hamilton and the other by Antonio. The map was old and it was a speculative treacherous journey. 20 local people were recruited who were experts in the local terrain. After everyone went through the map they said this Island was most likely close to the transit point opening near Sagar Dighi and Sundarban delta opening. We finally reached there. The weather was calm as we reached the place which looked like a mound on a vast opening of water, The soil seemed sticky. We had armed men with 303 Rifles as the excavation began. On the second night our team was attacked by two tigers which caused fatalities to three men. Yet the digging continued until on the fifth day the centre of the island started melting into water or at least as it seemed.

It was only after three hours of digging in the lantern light when two boxes were found. The boxes were unharmed and undamaged. However, there was something surrounding those boxes as well which was a mix of liquid and semi solid substance. The boxes were opened with great difficulty and when the boxes were opened gold seemed to be melting and stuck to the boxes. We wanted to moved the boxes away but the locals said they wanted more than 50 percent of the share. It was then when Hamilton had an idea. He said he is going to invest the wealth derived from here for the welfare of the people. I was surprised and asked that what made him sure that East India company would allow him to do that. He touched the sides of the boxes and said do you see this semi-solid substance. This is a mineral that can bring in more money once it's use is determined. The next few pages read on how the wealth was distributed between Antonio and Hamilton. In the last page it was written that Antonio removed one box and did not mention its whereabouts although Hamilton knew it was in another Island near Gosaba. Also, the East India company did not send any official to scout for the possible valuable mineral until. Fresh writing with new ink mentioning Barikul's name and a detailed map of the possible location of both the Islands.

CHAPTER FOUR

Project "Utopia"

It was around the remaining few days in December of 2022. Professor Biswas had been working at his home in the eastern part of Kolkata, specifically close to Salt Lake. It had been more than two years since the covid pandemic broke out that he had been working on "Project Global Assist". The idea behind the project was to build a global alliance and set out on two missions. The first was to establish alternative living space as earth became more and more unsustainable. The second one was to extract foreign and hidden pathogen both from earth and outside. It had been two years since he has been working on this global project. Only seven nations were involved. US, France, Germany, India, Israel, Japan and South Korea. The idea was to cultivate a proper research data on all the possible pathogens that could cause global pandemic. There has been a rumour that China, Russia, North Korea and Turkey were working on a certain project of their own which was meant as their own work on global bio warfare preparation and security against pandemics. Two years had passed by and Professor Biswas whose full name is Agniban Biswas. He had been a professor of space life and bio chemistry. His work had been on the discovery of pathogen which can cause global havoc and that included work on alien materials including rocks, pathogens etc. His work on creating a data set had been completed up to the extent of a quarter.

Since the days of pandemic, there was an initiative for join research and collaboration which had been kept a secret. There was a general belief that the human society was at the brink and there was a looming threat of a bio war. Out of this fear a core group of 7 member countries were invited on the side-lines of UN General Assembly. Prof. Biswas was heading the scientific committee on covid studies from the health ministry of India. It was here that he first had a meeting with the other 6 counterparts. Also, he met the heads of state including his own and the intelligence agency heads. There was something that he heard for the first time in this meeting which seemed straight out from Sci-Fi but was conveyed by US (FBI, CIA) and backed by Mossad as well as French DGSE and Germany intelligence agency too. They reported that it is apparently speculated that China was involved in bio-spreading covid through a lab leak. The initial plan was to leak a lower-level mutant and spread it from there to countries outside China. Russia was also aware of this plan and so was North Korea. It is said that Russia wanted to vaccinate its population against a lower-level infection of Covid while its mutants would be allowed to spread over the eastern part of Europe especially Ukraine, Finland, Sweden etc. However, the next part of the plan was more sinister which involved creating immune human population force.

The original reports of the preliminary study were not made available to the U.N. but the general observation report was made available to us. It was a report that gave details of all the lab experiments, virus composition.

However, the meeting brought out certain interesting facts. It could be clearly seen that the Chinese and the Russians had already started working on their vaccine projects much earlier than what the world had done. There was a power point presentation which was strictly for our eyes. It revealed certain things which was unbelievable and seemed to be more like a conspiracy until a point of time. However then came the shocking revelation. The presentation was made by the joint intelligence chiefs of all the seven countries including India. The report presented an idea which seemed improbable in the evening but was presented. It showed that the Chinese and the Russians through International Space Station had been working on two objectives. The first one was the collection of pathogens from the space. It was the second point that seemed improbable but got us more concerned. The slides 25-28 of the 50-slide presentation mentioned that Russia and China had been looking to establish connection with alien life. Now before one could raise question on this laughable concept, the next two slides mentioned that since 2017-2020, Russia and China along with North Korea had been working on establishing radio communication with life outside the Earth. However, the real success in 2022 after a specific incident.

Russian Spacecraft Soyuz had a mishap with fuel leakage. It was widely reported in the media as such. However, US, Space Force which monitors extra-terrestrial threats had found some unique signatures before the incident. Not only that radio frequencies for high range communication were also detected by US and European space agency apart from India. There has been communication found from China at the highest frequency since 2019. Also, certain energy signatures were found that carried signals of life which were not from the earth possibly. The heat signatures resembled something which was not uniform in terms of their energy traces. Some of them were quite high and some were significantly quite low. It was detected that at specific points since the covid crisis and later the Ukraine conflict the energy signatures would be found. In between there was another unverified correlation that was brought to the notice. It was found that every time a North Koran rocket launch was planned, the Chinese and the Russian space exploring pods close to each other. However, I and others in the team were still confused that how come this speculation was being observed at. That confusion was cleared in the last remaining slide. It was found out that every day based on rocket launches of North Korea the missiles original distance was kept low. However, as it was thought to be a technological fallacy of the North Koreans was actually being directed by the Chinese and the Koreans to musk up real intention.

The month of February 2021 was for the first time when rockets were fired from North Korea which the world media saw as provocation towards Japan or South Korea. However, the US Space Force had been picking up transmissions on each and every single day North Korean missiles were launched from around that time. The report mentioned that the speculation was there but to be absolute sure of a pattern that there was an establishment of communication between extra-terrestrial life and nations such as Russia, China along with North Korea seemed to be on to something that seemed far-fetched. However, the pattern over the last one and half years has been compiled. The transmission ranges have bounced back off from the spacecraft Soyuz and the Chinese spacecraft. Not only that the last year had proven presence of alien biomaterials and the heat signature as well. Most importantly there was another development which was shared by the Israelis. Their space team has been able to crack two transmissions, one from China and the other from Russia. They were of significant length and included significant unintelligible and alien communication. Although the interesting part of the transmission had been the transcript of the Russians and the Chinese. It pointed to a significant amount of request to utilize the virus variants of Covid for world domination. Although at the briefing none could confirm that whether the unintelligible language was actually alien in nature or a cryptic language that could not be deciphered till then.

However as of our briefing was coming to a close and I was sipping into a cup of tea, the last few words started ringing in my ears. The Israeli and the US security chief pulled out another slide which showed that the North Korean missile launches even if thought to divert attention had more serious purposes. The Russians and the Chinese had been trying to use the short range North Korean ballistic missiles not only to divert attention but also, they had secretly been working on a strategy which was meant for a global bio war. Every alternate week, after the North Korean launches the Chinese fighter jets would encroach Taiwan, during that specific time period, Soyuz and Russian unit in International Space Station would go into over drive. Communication interception would be highest. However, the Russian and the Chinese signals were masked to come off from International Space station and the Chinese Fighter Jets moving into Taiwan. It could be later confirmed that the actual signals were coming off from near the 38th Parallel. There was a ghost site which could not be located but it was close to the Korean mountains deep in the North

Korean territory. However, all of this big cover up for a global war using such an elaborate arrangement seemed to miss a key point which only got established two days before this meeting. There was Islamic Republic of Iran who had joined this build-up and supplying them with drones especially to Russia.

The briefing had ended and I moved to the adjoining room where there was a meeting of the scientific committee. I was placed next to the French scientist, Julia Sauvaire who had been a close friend of mine since we had work together at Marie Curie Institute 3 yeas back. The conference session was on when I could feel, Julia thrusting something in my hand. I looked at it for a split second and figured that it was a USB drive. I did not dare ask her question as along with the drive was a small piece of paper that she left right in front of my sneakers. I just picked up and thrust it in my pocket as the conference carried on. It was on a strategic roadmap of national security and how could each countries participate to deal with it. There was also a special interaction by NATO bio-security specialist. All done and dusted I returned back to my hotel as I knew that I had to look at what Julia had given me. I opened the chit which read “Don’t trust anyone. Burn this once you read it. The rest of the details are in the USB drive. Go over the files and the video snippets. Rest of it should be all clear to you”. It all seemed so shrouded in mystery as I plugged in the USB drive and with bated breath started to look for the contents. The first was a video snippet from a laboratory.

There was a woman and the picture was grainy but then on closer introspection it could be gauged that it was none other than the one who had been dubbed as the “Bat Woman” or corona researcher from Wuhan. In front of her there were three men with their faces covered. However, judging by the skin tone it seemed that they were either from Europe or may be USA. The confirmation came later. There were multiple documents which were written in some encoded form but the transcripts were available. In footnote of all those transcripts there was a coordinate which pointed to the same location in North Korea. After about reading 15 of the 50 files on the USB drive it became clear that there was a secret program funded by CIA, Mossad, FSB and Chinese Agency that was looking at means to emphasize the next level of bio war and cull human population. The alliance although seemed unbelievable to me at first could not be ignored as I went through the other files which had detailed budgets, signature of many top intelligence officials including three communiques from Pentagon. I could not believe that how come Julia got hold off all this although it was not my primary concern. The rest of the folders marked as "Project UTOPIA" had details on how much of the bio-war should be initiated at levels, the launch phase of the vaccines, which geographic regions to target and the demographic segmentation of global population.

I came out for a quick smoke and started to think that what could be all this about. I had already gone through the first few files and was reading up till 20 after I came back from my smoke. The file was on a detailed plan to attack India titled "Scheme 13" and was about the profile of Indian cities, health care system and hell even sewage details, airport screening facilities etc. I knew, I had to escalate this up to the national security advisor. However, as I was about to close the laptop, I quickly scanned through a few of the other files and finally found that there was a name of a private security firm that had been in charge of many hits across Iraq, Afghanistan, Iran and across all parts of the world The name of the unit was "Chess Board". It had apparently around 64 members and 11 people to whom these team members reported. However, I still could not find the connection. I knew I had to get this connection. It was all down to Julia to whom I had to make that call and which I did. I called her but could not reach her. As soon as I came back to my room and had just bent over a bullet pierced the screen of my laptop. Next thing I know, I was back in Delhi at a conference room having known that Julia was also shot in the spine having been paralyzed.

I did not know whom to trust and what to do next. I decided to meet NSA advisor as I had personally known him since last 5 years. I could frame piece by piece at least piece a bigger picture where there were several loopholes but I was trying to build one. I was lost in all of these thoughts when the NSA chief came in and we hugged. It had been some time but he was happy to see me. He asked "the usual"? I, was pleasantly surprised and nodded as he rang the bell. A waiter came in and said two black coffees. As soon as he left, I was eager to begin and I started with all the details. I had hardly finished when he interrupted me only once and said that last week there had been three Russian murders which probably may add up to something. Also there has been an unidentified flying object which had gone over Kolkata and it could not be ascertained as to what was it. The Indian special covert group had also not been able to collect much information except for activating Julia who was not only a top scientist but also a DGSE agent and close to me, said Ajit as I used to address him on a first name basis. He said to meet him in three days' time and in the mean time he asked me to stay in a safe house located close to central secretariat enclosure.

I received a call from the NSA and was asked to meet the chief in half an hour's time. I could not understand the urgency. I reported in the room in the new room which has been arranged in the South Block as one could see the new parliament building structure coming up. I saw, Ajit a bit agitated as he said that he could get the French intelligence chief on board after having a telephonic meeting with him for over an hour. He said that his reports suggest that a far-right US group with assets having close access to the White House has been parallelly funding a bio war. The Chinese had got on board as they had been targeting to spread the virus in around India. However, to avoid suspicion the Chinese started to slowly spread it from their mainland towards their neighbours and you know what was the first target for a severe population cull. The Russians were involved in the second phase who made a secret deal with the Turkish to use it for curbing any chance of dissent for their domestic problems. However, the master stroke was to divert the attention towards North Korea being actually controlled by the Chinese, Russians and US far right parallel group. To avoid suspicion the group arranged for 1000 drones ordered from Iran that had been smuggled to the target countries such as Ukraine and then from North Korea to South Korea and finally from around Iran towards Israel and Saudi,

I could now understand that what was all those files about as I recalled that the folders were divided into four sections. One was the phases, the second was the targets, the third were the routes and the fourth was the attack modes. As soon as I finished saying this, Ajit received a call. He listened to it pensively and then after he disconnected the call he turned towards the TV set and turned it on. Then instead of switching over to the TV channels he went straight up to the chrome and typed in Kolkata. I was perplexed for a moment to see what it was all about related to my city. Then I saw him trying Kolkata news and on the first page, I could see that there was news of an unidentified flying object over Kolkata. Ajit looked at me and then we quickly shared a lot of communication without saying a word. The USB drive that I had received from Julia in its fourth phase had talked of the payload delivery. It was through small missile carriers that looked like burning flames. It was designed as a payload delivery that emitted low level virus discharge under the garb of a fast flashing forward burst of light. Now if India was already being targeted in the post pandemic phase in a new manner, then the question remained what could we decipher from the USB drive for getting a certain idea. However, there was another question.

The mystery surrounding the death of three Russians was the topic that Ajit brought up. He said that IB has been trying to gather data along with R&AW. The latest news and the event of the unidentified flying object over Kolkata is something that can add up to something sinister. We were wondering about all of this when personal secretary of Ajit told him that he had a call on his secure line and it was urgent. He went to the other room and after about 5 minutes. I was called and the Video Conference was on. There was Julia from her hospital bed, DGSE Unit Chief, CIA, Mossad and WHO deputy head. I did not know that whether I fit in the bill of all these high-profile dignitaries. The door was closed. Julia started to speak as she broke down the details of Project UTOPIA. She said it would not have been possible without a data scientist of Huawei who was a French asset. He said that for long-time messages were transmitted from data centres of Huawei to government units to keep a track on the vaccination. Also, the zero covid policy was initialized around the same time Russia got involved in Ukraine conflict. This was done to keep the West busy with Ukraine-Russia war when China decided to exert influence of power on India and Taiwan. To broaden the alliance, Iran was backchannelled and being prepared for a quite conflict in West Asia and cull its domestic disturbances.

To spread global disorder being led from China and Russia, the aerosol-based virus was now being targeted across air in dense regions. The latest capsule-based projectile which had flown over Kolkata is actually targeted to spread the virus through air over regions North East especially Arunachal Pradesh and get in to the direct conflict. Russia is also looking to launch missile-based virus projectiles as they have been taking a hit. However, amidst of all this Julia pointing to CIA chief and Mossad head said there are right wing elements in US who had been secretly in collusion with Chinese agents especially posed as tourists to spread to areas which are populated with minorities. The same scenario is in Israel where right wingers apparently are using small apparatus to transmit them through smuggling routes across Jordan. In between she said that now is time to strategize our response against this global scenario. Then she looked at me and said that she can arrange for a few samples from the Chinese asset and send the sequence for an antidote development. Julia said that if they cannot stop the spread in the next three months then the whole scenario can be problematic as North Korea had prepared as well to launch these aerosol rockets across Japanese and Korean peninsula. To avoid radar and confuse air defences, the Russian and the Chinese satellites and their placement in ISS had been developing way to jam signals and obstruct communication and misunderstand objects of global threats.

I had texted Julia half an hour back the next day and asked her in person that I needed to get in touch with the asset. She denied that it was impossible, however she promised that she would get me a secure line to speak to him for about half an hour. Julia called me precisely by the time she promised and I was in a secure network going over call with a man introduced as Huawei. I did not probe further as he gave me specific details on when the Project UTOPIA started. It was meant to be an operation much like Eugenics of Nazi Germany an creating a new world order. The operation had begun since the fall of WTC and moved to the phase of implementation since 200 financial crises. The CCP core committee along with Russian Oligarch group had been on this since 2009and by 2013-2015 they had planned their plan of action. Since 2017 they had activated their financial strategy and activated their plan points. The Russian hackers with the help of Chinese and North Koreans had activated plans to back Trump, disrupt air defence systems of US and NATO. Last but not the least since 2019 the North Korean missile plan was activated which Julia must have told you about said Huawei. He said that they are going to launch virus every year through their population in China and move it around the globe. Meanwhile their ally assets program would do the other work.

That included creating havoc through right wingers in US domestic politics. Saudi has kept it as a backup for covert war on Qatar and UAE to establish their supremacy in Gulf Trivalry. Russian forces have also been injected with milder versions of Virus and an antidote and asked specifically to target populated areas in Ukraine to spread it from there to Europe creating refugee crisis through war. Last but not the least about India rest of the information has already been passed on to the National Security Chief. I asked what role I could play. He said that I needed to work on a mass vaccination booster program right now and steer clear of WHO for now as it may have been compromised. I asked him that why can't we make it public. He said its risky as the Project UTOPIA stakeholders may have infiltrated high profile assets and establishments all across. However, it would not harm if the news was spread from an alternative news source preferably a digital one. It could be then sold as "Conspiracy Theory" although it has truth. People who would want to believe having access to it can be prepared for vaccination without mass panic and affecting stock or financial markets which the Project UTOPIA stakeholders would want. Meanwhile your team can get going with the genome sequence sent by Julia to your NSA Chief and the French, Indian as well as Israeli team can collaborate and inform MI6, Australian intelligence too. He disconnected the call as Julia gave me a smirk and told her I would call her back, Meanwhile, I called my brother who worked as an investigative journalist for his news start-up Fire Arrow News and said "I have a story"

Printed by Libri Plureos GmbH in Hamburg, Germany